Nature vs. Nurture

AMY LAURENS

OTHER WORKS

SANCTUARY SERIES

Where Shadows Rise
Through Roads Between
When Worlds Collide

KADITEOS SERIES

How Not To Acquire A Castle

STORM FOXES SERIES

A Fox of Storms and Starlight
A Stag Of Hope And Memory

SHORTER WORKS

April Showers
Darkness And Good
Dreaming Of Forests
It All Changes Now
Of Sea Foam And Blood
Rush Job
Trust Issues

NON-FICTION

How To Write Dogs
How To Theme
How To Create Cultures
How To Create Life
How To Map
The 32 Worst Mistakes People Make About Dogs

Find other works by the author at www.amylaurens.com

Nature vs. Nurture

INKLET #53

AMY LAURENS

Inkprint
PRESS
www.inkprintpress.com

Print ISBN: 978-1-925825-55-8
eBook ISBN: 9781393836094

www.inkprintpress.com

National Library of Australia Cataloguing-in-Publication Data
Laurens, Amy 1985 –
Nature vs. Nurture
46 p.
ISBN: 978-1-925825-55-8
Inkprint Press, Canberra, Australia
1. Fiction—Science Fiction—Genetic Engineering 2. Fiction—Short Stories

First Print Edition: March 2021
Cover photo © Enrique Meseguer via Pixabay
Cover design © Inkprint Press
Interior art © Amy Laurens

NATURE VS. NURTURE

Sasha RECLINED INDOLENTLY IN THE chair opposite my classroom desk, cracking gum behind strawberry-bright lips, dark eyes staring from under her bottle-blonde hair through the window to the carpark beyond (loved my classroom view, so comforting and natural, nothing like having the best room in the whole school, ha).

Never had a school uniform looked so disreputable.

Sasha's mother Alison leaned forward to make sure she had my full attention (which, it was impossible not to hold someone's attention with hair that obviously fake, but hey, who am I to judge). "I'm sure it was simply a mistake," she said in that saccharine shade of politeness that went right out the other side to rude.

I managed to contain a sigh, and valiantly restrained myself from rubbing at my forehead. "I assure you," I said, straining for politeness as I shifted in my wheelie chair, "there's been no mistake. I'd be happy to provide you with copies of Sasha's assessment tasks if you'd like to see them. The ones she handed in, anyway."

Alison glared down her perfect nose and drummed her perfect, inch-long, scarlet nails on my chipboard desk. "What do you mean, the ones she handed in?"

This time I did sigh. "Mrs Young, surely you received the"—*numerous*—"emails I send home, and the letters, about Sasha's essay in first term and her creative just this month?"

"You should have kept her in," Alison pronounced.

Oh, yes, because I have nothing better to do with my lunchtimes than babysit your brat while she does nothing. I smiled thinly. "We tried that. For a week. Nothing was forthcoming, if you recall."

Further glares. "My Sasha is a good girl." Alison put her hand on Sasha's shoulder.

Sasha's glance flicked ever so briefly to her mother's hand, then to me.

When she realised I was looking straight back at her, she held my gaze, as if daring me to comment.

I filed that one away for future examination. Sasha was usually the touch-me-and-die type, and she didn't strike me as one to make allowances for her parents.

"I'm sure she is, Mrs Young." Deep down. Way deep down. "Which is why

I have no doubt that, if you wish to see her grade for this semester improved, she will hand in the two missing assignments." I transferred my gaze back to Alison, who, apart from the second chin, could have stepped straight out of a magazine with a title like Country Vogue.

"Usually the late penalties would mean that she would receive a zero for the tasks, but in this case I'm sure we could see our way to moving her up from a D to a C overall if the tasks were of sufficient quality."

Any second now, my brittle smile was going to crack.

"A C? A C! I didn't pay for my daughter to get Cs!"

I opened my mouth for a cutting retort about school fees, but Alison continued.

"I can't believe this." Her diction had slipped and I got the impression she was no longer talking to me. "We paid a *fortune* for her and the Association *promised* us we'd got the best genes there were. Top of her year, they assured us, no problems. And instead we get this ridiculous nonsense—" She broke off abruptly with a glance at Sasha, as though just remembering she was in the room.

Sasha maintained her bored stare out the window, but I thought I could see a tension in her jaw that hadn't been there before, a slight twitch behind the deep facade of flawless, on point makeup.

...And if Alison meant what I assumed she did, I didn't blame Sasha one bit.

I opened my mouth, considered my words, closed my mouth, and tried again. "Mrs Young," I ventured. "Do you mean to say Sasha was—is—a PAM baby?"

Sasha flinched at the term, and I resolved not to use it again. It was a whole lot less direct than the other terms people used—designer babies, GMs, or if the speaker was feeling particularly cruel, Chihuahuas, after the dogs a certain type of women back in the early decades of the century carried around in their handbags—but while the acronym 'PAM' wasn't so bad, it stood for Pick-And-Mix, and I supposed that wasn't really a friendly phrase either. I winced. I'd apologise to Sasha later, I supposed.

Alison had the good grace to look flustered, her grey eyes darting here and there, avoiding direct contact with me. "I thought you knew," she said, clutching her black Gucci vegan-leather bag. "You should have known! We told the school when we enrolled her! I specifically asked for that information to be disseminated to her teachers." Somewhere in her speech she'd gone from embarrassed to accusatory, and I bristled in response.

"No," I said. "I didn't know."

I made a show of glancing at my watch—a baby blue kids' one I'd found in an antique novelties shop for a couple of bucks. "I'm sorry but I have another meeting to get to. We'll have to continue this conversation another time."

I swept Alison up despite her protestations and escorted her out the door.

✄

"Did *you* know?" I asked Georgie, Sasha's year coordinator, as I sipped on some peppermint tea in the staff-room. The steam from it wafted over my face, the smell sharp and incisive.

Georgie shrugged and leaned back in the tattered gold arm chair—the most coveted teacher-spot in the school. "Of course. But admin thought she deserved the chance to go through school like a normal kid, so they didn't tell anyone. I only knew because I was there for her interview."

"Heh," I said, taking another sip and staring thoughtfully at the corner where the wall met the roof, mustard-coloured paint cracking away to reveal the gyprock underneath. "That must have been a barrel of laughs."

Georgie gave me a dark look. "You have no idea."

Actually, though, I kind of thought I did.

⬤

Sasha confronted me at the end of class the next day, waiting until the other students had filed out before hauling herself out of her back-row seat and sauntering toward me.

She stopped about half a foot closer than comfort and good manners allow-ed, and I breathed deeply, trying to remind myself that she had good reason to be belligerent about life.

"So, you gonna shut me in the back corner of the classroom now and let me do my own thing?"

I raised an eyebrow, pretty sure that I'd handled the lesson we'd just had the same way I always did.

Then something clicked. "Do you want me to?"

She fidgeted—just a little, just a shifting on her feet, but it was enough to confirm my sudden suspicion.

I sighed heavily. "Look, Sasha, this isn't going to work." I sat on the edge of my desk, suddenly too tired to stand. "First of all, I'm not going to let you go do your own thing on my time just because you've decided to check out. Know what that means?" I waited for eye contact before I continued. "It means I'm not giving up on you. Sorry. And second of all, this is a crappy way to punish your mum."

She startled visibly at that, eyes darting to mine, wary.

Teenagers. Always think they're so subtle and no one understands them. Oy. I smiled wryly. "It wasn't really hard to figure out, kid. She obviously treats you—" I'd be going to say like a show dog, but that was probably a little harsh, even if it was true.

I shook my head. "I get that you hold her responsible for your life and that there's more than a little resentment there. But this isn't the way to fix things. What are you going to do when you graduate with failing grades? Go cut grass for a living?"

She raised her chin, the fluorescent lights glinting off the tiny silver stud in her left nostril. "Nothing wrong with cutting grass."

"Yeah, and I hear it's a super interesting and engaging profession, too." I gave her a *look*.

Her lips twitched like maybe she'd

once dreamt of a smile. It was about five times more positivity than I'd ever seen from her before; I'd take what I could get.

I handed her the creative task she was supposed to have handed in three weeks ago that I'd re-copied earlier in the staffroom with Georgie. "Don't do it for her," I said. "Do it for you."

Sasha took the paper and shrugged. "Yeah," she said. "We'll see."

Yes, I thought as she left the room. Yes, we would.

THE MAKING OF *NATURE VS. NURTURE*

I have a feeling that one of those genetically-altered-humans films like *Gattaca* or some such had been on the curriculum recently when I wrote this story; I have vague recollections of sitting down to write this story with nothing particular in mind, and watching as it collided with the idea of designer babies that had been on my radar because of... something.

I'm also not quite sure *when* I wrote this story, but I have a feeling it was the year I was on maternity leave with my daughter.

This is because the classroom described in the story is my classroom from the school I was teaching at while

pregnant with her—quite a nice classroom, actually, despite the view of the
carpark!

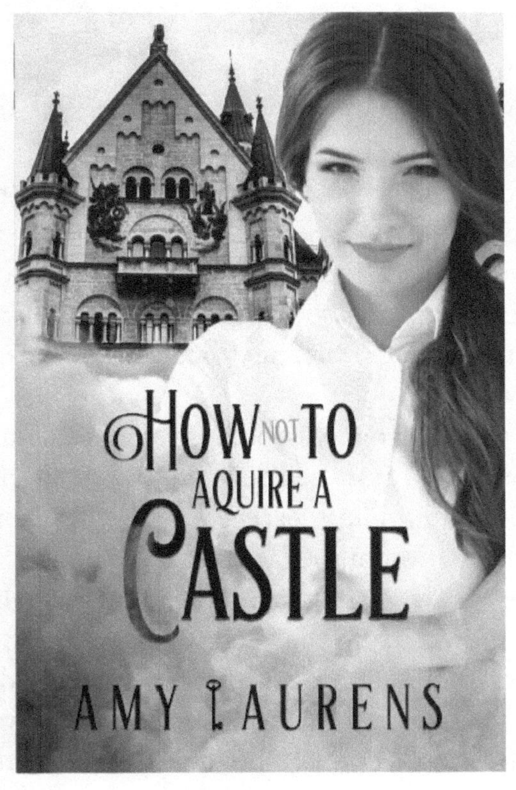
HOW NOT TO
AQUIRE A
CASTLE
AMY LAURENS

HOW NOT TO ACQUIRE A CASTLE

CHAPTER ONE

ON A HARD PLASTIC CHAIR IN THE FRONT row of the Great Hall in the world's fifth-best evil overlording academy, with its red-wooden parquetry floor that spoke of wealth and the beige, square panels of sound-boards speaking of conservatism on the walls, Mercury sat, pointedly not sweating.

Partly, this was because the Academy Administrators had deigned to turn on the air-conditioning earlier in the day, in recognition of the fact that the hall would be packed out with approximately six hundred bodies, all here to celebrate the graduation of about a third of that crowd.

But mostly, Mercury was pointedly not sweating because she made it a point never to sweat, sweat being an indication that she was working hard, and hard work being antithetical to her way of life.

However. If she *had* been sweating right now, it would not have been due to the uncomfortable warmth of six hundred packed bodies that even the air-conditioning system couldn't completely shift, or, in fact, from overexertion.

Instead, it would have been caused by an even more unfamiliar concept in Mercury's emotional vocabulary: nervousness.

Mercury did not *get* nervous. Mercury got things *done*.

So the fact that she was sitting here, in the front row of the Great Hall, about to graduate from Evil Overlording Academy (with distinction), and was feeling *nervous*… She crumpled the black paper program in her pale fists. It made her furious, that's what it did.

Abjectly furious, that snooty-tooty Deviran with his stupid morals and his stupid I-don't-want-to-be-here and his stupid Overlords-are-empty-figureheads and his stupid face sitting ten people over, looking implacable with his deep brown skin and barely-there, precision-groomed beard, as though he knew it gave him a stupid air of alluringly stupid mystery…

Mercury scowled and searched for the train of thought that had been derailed, yet again, by Deviran's stupidity.

Ah. Yes. She was angry because she was nervous because she wasn't absolutely entirely one hundred and fifty percent sure that she'd beaten Deviran in their final exams, and 1) being anything less than a hundred and fifty percent certain of anything made her cranky, and 2) being beaten by Deviran for dux of the year would be utterly unbearable. She flicked away a piece of fluff that had become snagged under her immaculately magenta-painted nails and smoothed out the black paper program.

In the front corner of the hall, the starkly-attired string quartet with their traditional black instruments began playing the March of the Oncoming Doom. The screechy scrapes of hundreds of chairs on the hall's wooden floor sounded as the crowd climbed to its collective feet.

Mercury sat with her arms firmly folded for a few moments longer, until her best friend Sparky kicked her in the ankle.

"Get up, idiot," Sparky hissed, hints of real flame flickering through her flame-coloured pixie cut.

"No," Mercury said, flouncing to her feet and tossing her own glossy brown hair back over her shoulders. Four years she'd been playing by the Academy's rules in order to get what she wanted, and she'd had just about enough. Other people's rules should only be applied to plebs too stupid to invent their own.

Sparky rolled her eyes somewhere over Mercury's head before focusing on the stage, where the ceremonial party had begun entering.

Mercury clenched her jaw and narrowed her own eyes as the teachers of the Evil Overlording Academy filed onto the stage, dressed in their formal finery. Each teacher had their own distinctive look that matched their personality and their Overlording style, from severe charcoal suits to jet-black leathers, pastel ballgowns and gem-toned lingerie and eye-blinding spandex, and even on one tiny old woman at the back, worn jeans and a grey flannel shirt. She was the one to watch out for, of course; Mercury could respect an Overlord who was confident enough in their abilities that they didn't need to telegraph them. It wasn't a look *she* would consider, of course, but still. She could respect it.

The band's march finished and, after a moderately awkward pause, the crowd sat. The Principal, pale skin and dark hair matching his suspiciously vampiric red-and-black suit, took the podium, and Mercury narrowed her eyes. He was doing a superb job of hiding his emotions—he was a premier Evil Overlord, after all—but she was Mercury, and unlike anyone else, she had the benefit of being able to rummage through people's consciousnesses. She was better at adding things *into* people's minds than taking information out, but he was telegraphing fear loudly enough that she could sense it without trying overly much.

Mercury pursed her lips.

Hmm.

The Principal cleared his throat at the blackened-wood podium, and the fear made it into his usually-unreadable eyes. "Before we begin," he said, and Mercury's stomach did a peculiar kind of flip-flop. "I have a pressing announcement to make regarding the safety of our students and their families."

He cleared his throat again and took out a sheet of paper from his pocket, unfolding it carefully and smoothing out the creases before beginning again. "The Council"—quiet booing echoed around the hall, and Mercury tsked impatiently— "have asked me to recommend that students from Tumul Tuos seriously consider postponing their return to town for a few days. The city is dealing with a *situation* at present which may present a danger to our students' health and safety."

Mercury's hands fisted at her sides and she forced herself to remain seated. What was wrong with her city? What had the Council mucked up now? A risk to the students' safety? There had to be more he wasn't telling them. Gently, Mercury tugged on his consciousness, implanting the suggestion that it might be better to share the news than to keep it secret. After all, how could they fight an enemy they didn't know?

"There are, ah..." He trailed off, glancing side to side as though wondering why his mouth had decided to continue.

Mercury didn't snicker, but she did press her lips together in satisfaction.

The Principal took a deep, steadying breath and seemed to change tack. "There has been one death already. The family have already been notified, so it is with much regret that I must inform you that Woovermyer will no longer be with us at the Evil Overlording Academy."

Murmurs broke out around the room, not all of them sad—to be expected in a school devoted to raising the next generation of dictators (ish) and despots (of sorts).

Mercury, however, crushed her program in her left hand, fist so tight her nails bit her palm.

"You okay?" Sparky murmured.

Mercury gave a single, tense shake of her head and stared at the podium. Dead. Livie Woovermyer was dead in *her city*. And the Council hadn't done anything to stop it. Couldn't do anything to stop it, probably, given they'd warned the students to stay away. Livie hadn't been the strongest candidate in the year level, but she was no lightweight, either. It would take a lot of power to kill a Seven.

Enough was enough. A good thing Mercury was about to graduate at the top of the class, giving her the right to knock the lowest ranking current Overlord off their perch. Tumul Tuos would be hers in a matter of hours. And then there'd be no more of these wasteful deaths. Her city would be safe at last.

Madame Pompadour was up the front now, elbow gloves the same glimmery silver colour as her elaborate, piled-curls wig, eyelids gleaming with matching silver eye shadow, and abruptly Mercury realised Madame was there to make the announcement that would change her life forever. She leaned forward in her seat, ready to stand when her name was called.

"And now the announcement you've all been dying for," the Political Alliances teacher trilled, the frills on her evening gown fluttering as she moved. "The dux of this year's cohort!"

Sweat slicked Mercury's palms. Irritated, she reached over and wiped them on Sparky's thigh.

Sparky pushed Mercury's hands back into her own personal space bubble and Mercury, nervous to the edge of distraction, let her.

"Will you please join me in welcoming to the stage, our wonderful dux for this year, Deviran Goodsmith!"

Mercury froze halfway to standing. "Did she just say Deviran?" she whispered furiously to Sparky.

Sparky hauled her forcibly back down into her seat. "Yes," she hissed back. "Sit down, you're making a fool of yourself."

Mercury's spine snapped upright as she sat, and she arranged the folds of her long black skirt demurely. "No I'm not." She closed her eyes. "Deviran's going up to the stage, isn't he?" Even at a whisper, the misery in her voice was clear, but this time, she didn't care.

Sparky reached over and squeezed her hand.

Mercury squeezed back, lacing her fingers through Sparky's, and held tight as all her plans and dreams vanished in front of her.

A stone had landed in her chest. That must be it. Some strange sort of magic that made her chest contract and sink, and made the world distort for just a moment, long enough to trick her into thinking Deviran had beaten her so that someone could jump in front of her and yell SURPRISE!

Any moment now.

Any moment.

She refused to open her eyes and watch Deviran parading across the stupid stage like some stupid stupid-person, receiving his stupid medal and stupid symbolic crest pin.

It was that last exam question.

She'd known Deviran would pull out his ridiculous 'Evil Overlords are merely figureheads, the Business Guild is where the power really lies' rant that everyone had heard a million times back when he was younger and angrier, and she'd tried to counter it, she really had.

She'd argued for the importance of the Overlording position, for the power of having a symbolic figure to unite the population in their hatred, for having a person able to make all the difficult, necessary decisions the Council was too weak and spineless to make… But it hadn't been enough. Everything she'd worked for, everything she'd set out to prove—and it wasn't enough.

There were words, there were names, and then forever later, once she'd died twice already, Sparky elbowed her in the ribs. "Come on," Sparky muttered. "We're up next."

And sure enough, there was a shuffling of presenters as the last of the Powers Behind The Thone graduates departed the stage, and the next speaker announced in threatening, funereal tones, "The Over-lording cohort."

Mercury blinked furiously and followed Sparky to the end of the line at the right side of the stage. The other candidates proceeded one at a time across the stage, two girls and then stupid Deviran, and then a handful more and then Sparky, and then the speaker was calling her name.

Hands fisted, Mercury tossed her head high, climbed the four steps, and marched across the stage. She wouldn't look at them, the stupid faculty who'd denied her the city she rightfully deserved, and she wouldn't look the other way either, at the classmates and crowd undoubtedly sniggering at her failure.

She shook hands with the presenter, and while he pinned the tiny crossed-swords badge on her collar, her eyes betrayed her and slid towards the audience. Her stomach flipped as she saw the crowd of parents and friends behind the rows of students, all the way to the back of the hall, twenty rows at least, illuminated by the late afternoon light streaming in through the ceiling-high windows to the right. Everyone had someone here to watch them graduate. Everyone except Weird Al—and her.

The presenter finished with her pin, muttered something to her, and offered his hand again. Mercury coldly ignored it and strode from the stage. It didn't matter. None of it mattered. Tumul Tuos was her city anyway, and no one could change that. She'd think of something. She'd take a day or two out, make some plans…

And she could always hope that Deviran would choose some other Overlording territory. He'd be stupid to, but then again, he was stupid, so. Mercury could hope.

All at once, mid-way down the steps off the stage, Mercury came to rigid attention, scanning the room. Somewhere out there in the crowd, an exchange of power had just taken place, and it felt… unusual.

But the final few students were backing up behind her and muttering, so Mercury headed back toward her seat, craning her head all the while and searching for some sign of whatever it was that had just discharged a dizzyingly quiet amount of power into the room.

She sat, and Sparky leaned over. "Okay?"

"Mm," said Mercury. "Did you feel…" She accidentally caught the eye of the student behind her and twisted back to face the front.

"Feel what?"

Mercury turned it over in her mind. It had felt like a large shot of power discharged very quietly—but perhaps it hadn't been. Perhaps it had only been a small discharge after all, something most people wouldn't have noticed.

But still, something about it had tugged on her. It very nearly felt like something she'd felt before, only she *knew* she'd never sensed that kind of discharge before.

She shook her head. "Never mind. Don't worry."

Sparky sighed and straightened. "It's fine, Mercury," she said, drily exasperated.

"I know you didn't win, but I promise, you'll live through it."

Mercury waved a hand for silence.

The power had just discharged again, and it had come from somewhere in the back corner, far away from the windows and light.

Impatiently, Mercury waited for the formalities to conclude. The crowd stood while the quartet played the exit march, and the stage party left, Mercury tapping her foot all the while.

The moment the last notes of the march died away, Mercury turned and headed to the back corner, weaving in and out of the students and parents who had seemed to explode slowly but inexorably out from the neat rows of seating, ignoring Sparky's calls behind her. Power, something that tugged in a way that was strange and familiar, all at once. She pushed her way through a family posing for pictures—and halted.

In the shadows of the back corner, Deviran stood with his family, with his stupid, smug little smile, looking as tall and dark and stupidly alluring as ever. Prat.

His mother, short but sleek, and his father—tall, and utterly terrifying in a way not at all diminished by his gleaming smile—gushed over him, patting his back and hugging him tight. Within moments the Principal was there, glibly shaking hands and congratulating them on the success of their son. Something flickered across his consciousness, and also Deviran's father's—some moment of recognition in response to what they were saying.

But Mercury brushed it aside just as the mother brushed melodramatic tears from her cheeks and handed Deviran a silver-wrapped package about as long as her hand but half the width.

That. That was the source of the strange, magical feeling. Mercury watched hawk-eyed as Deviran un-wrapped the gift. A glimpse of gold set her pulse racing—What was it? What did it do? Could she steal it?—and then the paper fell away to the floor, and Deviran stood staring wordlessly at the object in his hands, and Mercury did too.

Wide-eyed, Deviran raised his gaze to his parents, and even from where she stood Mercury could hear the reverence in his voice as he thanked them.

But Mercury had eyes only for the object. No wonder she'd felt it discharge, and no wonder it had felt both strange and familiar. In Deviran's hands lay a glorious, sunshine-gold key, large and strong—and with a handle in the shape of a stylised fish, long, flowing fins curving to make the grip.

A Key. They'd given him a Key. And not just any Key, but *the* Key, *her* Key, the Artefact of Power belonging to *her* city.

A wordless noise of wanting rose in Mercury's throat. Who cared about being dux? She needed that Key.

Keep reading! Head to
www.inkprintpress.com/amylaurens/
kaditeos/castle/
to buy your copy now!

ABOUT THE AUTHOR

AMY LAURENS is an Australian author of fantasy fiction for all ages. While designer babies are not a Thing (yet), Amy has definitely encountered her fair share of parents just like Mrs Young.

Amy has also written the award-winning portal-fantasy *Sanctuary* series about Edge, a 13-year-old girl forced to move to a small country town because of witness protection (the first book is *Where Shadows Rise*), the humorous fantasy *Kaditeos* series, following newly graduated Evil Overlord Mercury as she attempts to acquire a castle, the young adult series *Storm Foxes*, about love and magic and family in small town Australia, and a whole host of non-fiction.

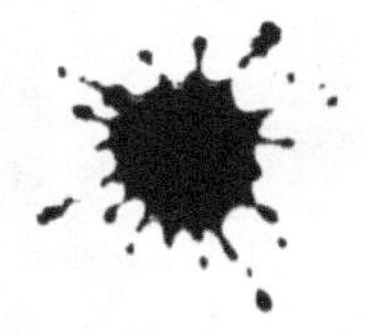

INKLETS

Collect them all! Released on the 1st and 15th of each month.

INKLET #055
Allure
AMY LAURENS

INKLET #056
The LIES We KNOW
LIANA BROOKS

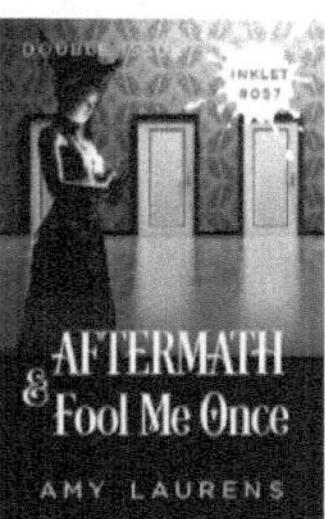

INKLET #057
AFTERMATH & Fool Me Once
AMY LAURENS

INKLET #058
Purity
An Age Of Unicorns Story
AMY LAURENS

INKLET #059
Saved
AMY LAURENS

INKLET #060
A Kiss is the Secret
AMY LAURENS

INKLET #061
A Changing Tides Story
Fire Bright
AMY LAURENS

INKLET #062
Hades AND Persephone
LIANA BROOKS

INKLET #063
Just So Long As You're Happy
AMY LAURENS

INKLET #064
Theft Of A Lifetime
LIANA BROOKS

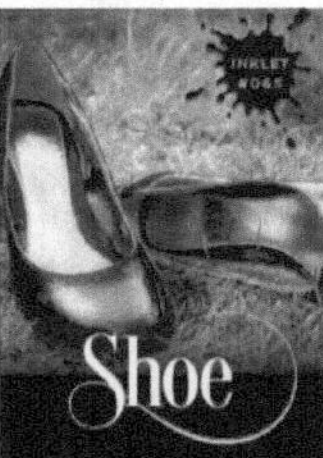

INKLET #065
Shoe
AMY LAURENS

INKLET #066
Published AUTHOR
LIANA BROOKS

DOUBLE ISSUE
INKLET #067
THE REMARKABLE INSIGHT OF JELLYBEANS & Understanding
AMY LAURENS

INKLET #068
Desperate Measures
AMY LAURENS

INKLET #069
Rock-a-bye
LIANA BROOKS

INKLET #070
the Other Carly
AMY LAURENS

INKLET #071
Bs By Bioluminescent Light
AMY LAURENS

INKLET #072
Even Villains Grant Wishes
A Heroes & Villains Story
LIANA BROOKS